Ladybird books are widely available, but in case of
difficulty may be ordered by post or telephone from:

Ladybird Books – Cash Sales Department
Littlegate Road Paignton Devon TQ3 3BE
Telephone 01803 554761

A catalogue record for this book is available
from the British Library

Published by Ladybird Books Ltd Loughborough Leicestershire UK
LADYBIRD and the device of a Ladybird are trademarks of Ladybird Books Ltd

DISNEY

Snow White
and the Seven Dwarfs

Ladybird

Once upon a time, there lived
a princess called Snow White.
Her father, the King, was dead.
Snow White lived with her wicked
stepmother, the Queen, in a castle
at the edge of a deep, green forest.

Snow White was very beautiful. Her
skin was as white as snow, her hair
as black as ebony wood and her lips
were as red as a red, red rose.

The Queen was also very beautiful
but terribly vain. She had a magic
mirror and every day she would look
into it and say:

> *"Magic mirror on the wall,*
> *Who is the fairest one of all?"*

The mirror would always reply:

> *"You, O Queen, are the fairest*
> *of them all."*

But the Queen was still jealous
of Snow White's beauty. She made
the Princess dress in rags and work
in the castle as a servant.

One day, after the Queen had spoken to her magic mirror, the mirror replied:

"Famed is thy beauty, Majesty,
But behold, a lovely maid I see.
Alas, she is more fair than thee,
Lips as red as a rose, hair as
    black as ebony,
Skin as white as snow."

The Queen was furious. "Snow White!" she hissed. "It cannot be!"

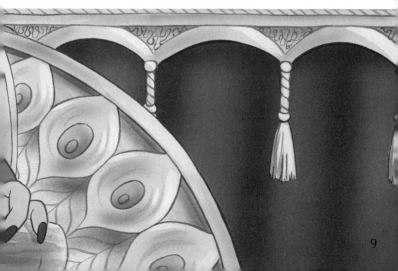

Just at that moment, Snow White was cleaning the steps at the castle well. While she worked she sang of meeting the true love of her dreams.

A handsome prince who was passing by stopped at the well to listen.

The moment the Prince and Snow White met, they fell in love.

When the Queen saw Snow White and the Prince together, she was filled with even more hatred for the Princess. She began to think of a plan to get rid of her stepdaughter…

The next morning, the Queen sent
for her huntsman. "Take Snow White
out into the forest," she ordered.
"I want you to kill her so I *never*
have to see her again."

The Queen told the huntsman to bring back Snow White's heart in a box to prove that she was dead.

The huntsman sadly led the Princess into the forest. He knew he could not kill someone who was so kind and innocent.

"Run away into the forest and hide," he told Snow White as he knelt beside her. "The Queen must think that you are dead – you must *never* return."

Then, the huntsman placed an
animal's heart in the box the Queen
had given him. The Queen had to
believe that Snow White was dead.

Horrified, Snow White ran off into
the forest. She was terrified by the
dark shadows and strange noises.

Soon, animals and birds gathered round to comfort Snow White. They led her to a little cottage, hidden deep in the forest.

Snow White knocked on the door and went inside. She wondered who could live in such a tiny house – everything was so *very* small!

There were seven dusty little chairs
at the table. In the sink there were
seven dirty spoons and bowls. And
in the bedroom there were seven
unmade tiny beds.

"Perhaps children live here," Snow
White said. "But how untidy
everything is!"

So, with the help of her forest friends,
Snow White dusted and cleaned the
little cottage. Then she went upstairs
to rest and soon fell fast asleep
across three of the tiny beds.

Evening came and the owners of the cottage returned from their day's work. They were seven dwarfs who worked in diamond mines, deep in the heart of a mountain. The dwarfs marched along singing:

*"Heigh-ho, heigh-ho,
It's home from work we go!"*

As soon as they entered the cottage, they knew that something was wrong – it was clean! The floor had been swept and there was a delicious smell coming from a pot on the fire. "What's happened?" they asked each other in amazement.

"Maybe it's ghosts," said one of the dwarfs in a trembling voice.

"Careful, men! Search every nook and cranny," said another.

Their search eventually led them up the stairs into their bedroom.

Just then, Snow White stirred and
woke up. "Why, it's a girl!" the dwarfs
gasped. "Who are you?" they asked.

"My name is Snow White," said the
girl. She explained why she was
hiding in their cottage. Then she
asked the little men, "Who are *you*?"

22

"I'm Sneezy."

"I'm Happy."

"And he's Dopey,"
they all shouted
together.

"I'm very pleased to meet you all," said Snow White. "If you let me stay here, I promise I'll look after the house for you. I'll wash and sew and cook." The dwarfs quickly agreed!

"Supper's not quite ready," continued Snow White. "You'll just have time to wash."

"I knew there was a catch to it," grumbled Grumpy. "Well, I'd like to see anybody make *me* wash!"

"All right," said Doc. And six dwarfs tossed Grumpy into the wash-tub and scrubbed him clean! Then they all enjoyed a delicious supper.

That evening, the little cottage was filled with music and laughter. The dwarfs sang and danced to welcome the Princess to their home.

Snow White was so happy that she soon forgot all about her wicked stepmother.

Meanwhile, the wicked stepmother was celebrating Snow White's death. But the next time the Queen said the special words to the magic mirror, the mirror replied:

> *"Snow White, who dwells with
>   the seven dwarfs,
> Is as fair as you and as fair again."*

The Queen was enraged. "Snow White must *still* be alive!" she screamed. "My huntsman has tricked me!" She vowed to get rid of Snow White once and for all…

Down in the deepest dungeon of her castle, the Queen cast a magic spell to disguise herself as an old pedlar woman. Then, she prepared a deadly gift for the Princess…

Chanting a magic spell, the wicked Queen dipped a bright red apple into a bubbling pot of poison.

"One bite of this and Snow White will fall into the sleep of death!" she cackled. "Only love's kiss can save her. But the dwarfs will think she's dead and bury her alive!"

The very next day, after the dwarfs
had left for work, there was a knock
at the cottage door. Snow White
opened it and saw an old pedlar
woman standing there.

The woman had a basket full of apples. "Try one, pretty maid," she said, smiling. "They are magic wishing apples – one bite and *all* your dreams will come true."

Thinking of the Prince she had met at the castle well, Snow White reached out for the red apple. She took a bite and fell to the floor.

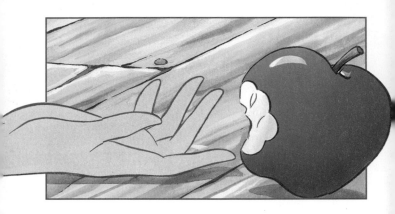

"Now *I'm* the fairest in the land!" cried the wicked Queen, before fleeing from the cottage.

Luckily, Snow White's forest friends had recognised the Queen and fetched the seven dwarfs for help.

As the dwarfs rushed towards the cottage, there was a crash of thunder and a mighty storm began.

Doc spotted the Queen running away. "Quick, after her!" he cried. The dwarfs chased her through the forest and up the mountain side.

The wicked Queen struggled ahead
with the dwarfs right behind her.
When she realised she was trapped,
she loosened a huge boulder and
started to push it towards the dwarfs.

But the boulder rolled backwards
onto the Queen. With a terrible cry,
she fell over the side of the mountain
never to be seen again.

When the dwarfs returned to the cottage, they found Snow White lying on the floor, as if she were asleep.

They tried everything they could think of, but Snow White could not be woken.

So, the seven dwarfs took the Princess into the forest. There, they built a special bed for her made of glass and gold. The dwarfs kept watch over her day and night.

The months slowly passed. Snow White's glass bed was covered with leaves, then snow, and then the blossoms of spring, and still she slept.

One day, a handsome young man came riding through the forest. He was the Prince who had fallen in love with Snow White by the castle well. When he saw the Princess, he got down from his horse, leant over her and tenderly kissed her.

All at once, Snow White's eyes fluttered open. "She's awake!" the dwarfs cried, excitedly. The wicked Queen's spell was broken!

* * *

Before Snow White left to begin her new life with the Prince, she kissed each of the dwarfs. "I'll come to see you very soon," she promised them.

The dwarfs watched the Prince
sweep his beloved Snow White up
into his arms. They knew they would
miss her but they also knew that she
and the Prince would live happily
ever after.